By

© Inakat 2013

© Inakat Publishing 2012

Detroit, MI

Book Cover Design By Inakat

ISBN 978-0-9883533-4-3

Dedication

To the Mixologist, Detroit's own DJ Base, a teacher, musician, entrepreneur, mentor, and father figure to many, you will always have unyielding gratitude, from your big headed baby...lol.

Contents

Big Body Base

Big Body Base

Chapter 1

"Mama and dad came and woke me up. Santa had eaten the milk and cookies that me, you, and mama made for him. Well, you didn't actually help make them. We let you hold the bag of chocolate chippies and you ate most them. I ran to the window to see if I could see Santa's sleigh. I didn't but I heard the bells from the reindeer. It was snowing so hard, I hoped that he made it to everybody's house safe.

The Christmas tree was all lit up and we live in that small apartment. Mama was still in the kitchen rolling and cutting the dough for more peach cobbler. Oh my goodness, the smell of the spices and sweet cream butter filled the air. I ran toward the biggest box and saw it had my name on it. I sat on the floor by the tree and started to rip the Charlie Brown wrapping paper off in big pieces.

I wanted to dance when I saw what it was. A drum set. A whole, complete, real drum set. It had a snare drum, tom-tom, bass drum, high hat, foot cymbal, two sets of drumstick, and an adjustable seat. It even came with keys to tune the drums and a foot pedal for the bass drum. It was Royal blue with shiny chrome trim. It took everything in me not to do the Electric Slide across Mama's freshly waxed hardwood floor.

Dad stayed up and helped me put it together. My hands shook a little when he gave me the sticks. Dad played the harmonica a little bit, Ma could sing and play the guitar, but me I fell in love with music right there in that living room. The only other time I'd been that close to a real drum set was the one they had at church. Dad didn't go with us, so I guess I must have talked his ears off about it because that what he got me for Christmas.

To m, it seemed like drums let the spirit flow in church. Every other instrument could stop. When the drums played, hands would clap almost by themselves, feet would stomp, praise would go up and it's like the Holy Ghost just tarried in that place for a while. Mama got that loud voice and she sang Acappella, that's without music. But towards the end of the song, when the musicians jumped in, she'd waved off everybody but the drums. You had to see it to understand. I seen it and I wanted to play them drums so much.

I can't exactly describe how come. It's like I was meant to play them. I didn't take lessons, we couldn't afford them and the drums. I think God wanted me to play those things. I could barely read my name and I surely couldn't read sheet music. I learned what they called " to play by ear" . That's is to listen, to imitate, and then to repeat it. That was a little hard though, especially behind live singers. There was no guarantee they'd sing the song the same way twice. Even at that,, I wanted it and I didn't get lucky, I was blessed." Thomas said.

Misty always thought her Thomas was modest about his talents. Her mother had taught her to sing. Her mother's own father had been a voice coach for Great groups such as the Five Blind Boys. Song, music, and spiritualism ran deep in the family bloodlines. Misty had only taken formal lessons to play the Clarinet years later, but the talent of music in the soul belonged to Thomas Base. As the years went by, he would pick up and master nearly every instrument in a way that few do. He did so in church and more importantly "by ear". By the time Thomas took formal training to read sheet music, he'd already been skilled in several instruments. Thomas has accomplished songwriting, music composing, and had shown an uncanny ability to sing in every voice from base to high tenor.

Thomas was a round, soft, huggable child, mocha brown-skinned with a thick dense afro, charming smile, pleasant, mild-mannered, and had a slight gap-toothed grin. Misty's laziness has been the cause of his chipped front tooth when he was ten. When it was her turn to clean up their toys, Misty had taken her Strawberry Shortcake fold up table and shoved it on a shelf in the closet. She closed the door on pile of toys and left it. When Thomas later opened the door the metal framed table flew down, popped him in the mouth, and chipped his front tooth. Although, Thomas appeared to be soft to others, he had the heart and sometimes temperament of "Rocky Balboa".

At the age of eleven, Thomas met his mentor, idol, confidant, and longtime friend. Thomas's own father was construction worker who rarely missed a days' work, which included Sundays. Mr. Sander Love, Music Director at Pelham Magnet, looked up from his desk one day, and saw that familiar thirst for the salvation that's found and shared by music lovers in the eyes of Thomas. He didn't fuss as his new little shadow fell into place and began the march towards leadership behind him. In fact he welcomed and helped shape him into one of the greatest leaders the city of Detroit would ever see.

Misty had often wondered if others saw what she'd seen. Thomas had been picked on for everything from his weight to his hair. At the age of ten, Thomas appeared to a man. He sported a matched size ten shoe and stood almost six feet tall. His voice and speech was the only clue that he was still a kid.

Thomas was born in late April of nineteen sixty nine. A decade later, the streets of Detroit were filled with litter, overdosed heroine addicts, the occasional body of a victim of drugs or random street violence and prostitutes on every other corner. Gangs were the daily norm and hip-hop and rap were on the rise. Liquor was cheap, racial tensions were high,, the drop-out rate for even higher and trouble lurked around every corner.

He'd overcome a speech impediment and what his mother thought to be dyslexia. In fact, Thomas wasn't dyslexic or slow, he just didn't like school that much. Until music that is. Once the kindergartener who got the boot for misbehaving, the threat of losing his drum set became the one factor that could get Thomas to fly right. He practiced on his speech daily at home with his family. One day it was no longer there. The transformation was so great, that he later went on to become a live on air radio personality for several radio stations in the local Detroit area.

The picture for a young, black male is an urban area like Detroit, could easily have been painted one of two ways. His face behind a prison bars sentenced to life or death row for a handful of drugs or in casket due to violence, drugs, or suicide. Many of the people that he'd grown up with died before their twenty fifth birthday or found themselves locked behind stone and steel.

He'd learned only on how to take torment and tune in around on those who tried to give it. He was known for his silly nature and quick wit. Thomas often hid the pain of his life as a source of strength and encouragement to others. Misty had always known that one day he'd be the man to make the difference. Even though some feared him because of his massive size, behind his back even Misty teased him ad the "gentle giant".

To have survived the darkness was rare. To march through it in the snow, wind, heat, and rain and bring passels of children with someone was even rarer. Thomas Base was the kid half the world wanted to be and the other half took as a joke. As a child he was dismissed as a chubby kid with a cute face. In an urban area where few males see success, he grew tired of hearing "try something else" from teachers and classmates alike. Armed with a passion for music and creativity, he literally took a local town by storm.

Chapter 2

The sound of raindrops in the window comforted Misty. It had been nearly four years since the funeral. The trial was about to start in two days. Misty gripped the umbrella firmly and checked her watch. She wondered if the sudden storm would lighten up before she made it out of Rockland.

When she received the call, Misty did her best not to scream. She'd woken up with a bad feeling in her stomach before the phone even rang. Once she'd been awakened with the news, Misty couldn't go back to sleep. She had packed her bags and waited for daylight to break, before she pulled out. It would be a long, quiet drive on 1-94 to get back to Michigan.

Misty Base-Jordan was a forty-nine year old woman. Her tall, lean body made her appear to be in her early teens. She'd worked as a waitress most of her life. She enjoyed people and conversation. Her mother had passed away when she was thirty years old. That left Misty, her brother, a sister she rarely spoke to and her brother, alone and estranged. She had other siblings from her father's first marriage, but they weren't close either.

Misty had married Scott Simpson when she was just twenty years old. They had three children together. Scott had been a cruel, mean-spirited man. For the sake of appearances, Misty had done what she could to hold the marriage together. However, an incident had caused Misty to pack only what she could carry and flee with the children in fear of their lives.

Misty had a three-year-old son, a two-year-old daughter, and was pregnant with their third child. At twenty-four years old, Misty left with them clothes on her back and a few things for the kids to start her live over. She'd been working as a bathroom attendant and cashier part-time and taking college courses to get her degree in Business Management.

Before she'd left, Misty had begged Scott for a divorce. He'd refused. Misty couldn't afford to file and care for the children without saving for it. Her husband had been making excuses not to work since three weeks after they'd married. Misty was the breadwinner and tired after three years. Scott kept after her to return to him, he'd claimed to love her and believed he was the only man that could make her happy.

The last time she'd Scott, he shown up at her grandmother's house. He'd said he just wanted to talk and see his kids. Misty listened while Scott went from telling her how much he'd love her to demands that she return to him. Again Misty refused and instead asked for a divorce. Misty spent the night at her grandmother's with the children that night.

The next morning, Misty awoke to loud knock at her grandmother's front door. She opened it to find Scott and a woman on the other side. He told Misty that he'd wanted her to met his pregnant girlfriend. Misty informed Scott that she didn't care and that she'd hoped now he'd give her a divorce. The woman interjected and Misty promptly shut her down.

"I don't know you and don't know me. Wait until you find out what you've got on your hands. I've children in the house to care for, so do us both a favor, take him on home with you. You wash his clothes, cook his meals, and perform my wifely duties. I'm not coming back to him. Whatever he's told you, whatever it is that you believe that has you standing on my grandma's doorstep go ahead on and believe it. I don't think to much of you already.

You're standing here to tell me you're pregnant and I just gave birth to his son three days ago. He never mentioned you or your baby when he was here last night. For all you know he brought you here to a house full of people that might hurt you while you're pregnant. It's shows how much he thinks of you. It would be funny, except that's the kind of man you're dealing with. Don't come back over here. It's not going to be pretty.

As for you Scott, tell her all those lies you told me last night. Or better yet, take her by Jackee's house and let her tell it for the both of us. How's her son doing by the way? I'm sure he's better off minus you too. I didn't get into with her and I ain't about to get into with you about him. You're knocked up by a married man, that just had yet another baby by his wife. I bet he's living in your house and puffing your head up with bullshit. You don't confront anybody over half the story. Some of these punks will get you hurt because they know they ain't hitting on much and they want somebody to act a fool over them." Misty said.

"He told me y'all was separated. He was over here last night? Jackee? Who's Jackee?" The woman asked.

Misty laughed before she shut the door. She'd felt a twinge of pity for the woman just the same. At least Scott had bothered to acknowledge that he'd married her. He'd never mentioned Jackee or her pregnancy to Misty. He'd simply told her that he'd a stop to make and drove her over to Highland Park.

Misty was in the car when he'd gone into the house. A few moment later, Scott ran out and began to kick the gate. A woman and several other people had come out too. The woman was pregnant and screamed.

"What are you going to do about the baby Scott? Are you going to help me or what? I don't care about you screwing some little high school girl. A grown woman wouldn't want you. I'm going to put you on child support Scott. You wasn't worried about her last night when you was over here in the bed with me. You can't live up in my house and not work. If you wanted to be with me, you would have get us a place like a man." She said.

Scott jumped in the car and pulled off. He told Misty that the woman was a slut he'd met in the middle of the night at a Coney Island. Afterwards Misty asked and Scott finally told her the woman's name. He'd sworn that he'd used a condom with her. He said he'd slept with her once and she tried to pin someone else's baby on him. Misty was already pregnant with their first child and foolishly believed him. Four years later, Misty realized that the woman had told the truth, about Scott at least.

Misty went to stay with her parents, until she could manage to get up on her feet. Scott found out and began to terrorize and stalk Misty. She'd began to fear that Scott would hurt her parents as well and Misty moved out into a place of her own. She only told her parents and a friend where she was.

Scott had used the children as a way of controlling Misty. He shown up at her friend's house Peach and demanded to know where Misty and the children were. Peach told Scott to leave her house. Scott was furious.

Scott had managed to use the court system and family connections to find out where Misty lived. He showed up on her doorstep and demanded that she and the children return to him at once. Misty said no. Three days later, while Misty was out with the children, Scott burned her house down.

Misty took the kids and vanished soon after. She remained in hiding with the children as long as she could. It seemed to Misty that no matter how much she'd tried to avoid Scott, he'd somehow find out where she was. Misty would then pick up and move in fear that the next time, she and the children would be in the house when Scott snapped.

The brother that she'd been the closest to had no idea she'd even left. The tragedy had taken it's toll on everyone.

However, Thomas Base had been disappointed. For him, it was if the sister he'd known had just disappeared. Misty had kept tabs on her family, but she didn't approach them or interfere in their lives.

Thomas, Misty's brother, was fours years older than her. He was what she'd imagined most guys she be like in terms of a mate. Misty had always depended on his solid character and style. Thomas adored both of his sisters, but his path in life was that of a self-made man.

Misty was only a year old when Thomas met his first love. It was a cold and icy Christmas morning. Their father James had doted on the children equally but with Thomas as the only other male in the house, he wanted to do something very special for his fifth Christmas. Misty couldn't remember it, but he'd told her the story a thousand times.

Scott had literally made sure that Misty was alone by his actions. He'd vowed that he'd take the children from her as well. He'd made plain his intentions to see Misty grovel at his feet. Misty decided that as long as her children were safe, she didn't care.

Now she had to go back to Detroit. She'd hadn't planned to stay. Once she paid her respects and saw a few people, Misty would return to her quiet little corner in life and leave her past behind her. The children were finally grown and she'd no reason to be there. Scott's hold on her life had been the kids and now they too lived in Detroit.

Since they'd decided to join their father, Misty took it a sign that her mission was complete. Despite the intense effort to see Misty labeled as Abandoned Property, Scott actions had actually put her in a better position. Misty had suffered in silence so long that she'd become numb. She was relieved that she now she'd have the chance to heal and do something she'd never thought to do. Live.

Chapter 3

Misty stood up from the Lazy boy chair and walked toward the door. She picked up her purse and keys from the coffee table, before she grabbed her suitcase. As Misty touched the door handle, she tried to remember if she'd had left anything unattended in the house.

Satisfied that she hadn't forgotten anything, Misty locked the inside handle of the door and made her way to the car. It was less than three minutes later when the car was packed, Misty drove up East State St., and headed towards the I-80 entrance. The rain had picked up. She suddenly wished that also remembered to bring along her raincoat, just in case.

When Misty passed the Alpine Hotel, she bit her bottom lip. Every time Misty passed there, it brought back a flood of memories. Unfortunately, the long drive ahead would give her plenty of time to think. The sight of the hotel had become an emotional landmark for her.

Misty felt her cheeks warm at the thought of what had happened there. Instead, she willed herself to concentrate on the road. She looked up just in time to see the red taillights of other vehicles as they approached the Elgin Toll. Misty dug in the side door and picked out a quarter and a nickel to pay the thirty-cent toll. In a few moments, she had paid her fee and rolled back into the flow of traffic.

She would be glad to see her family again except for the circumstances. Her friend, Vera had lost a child. She didn't know what she do a part from be there for her. Before Vera had a chance to grieve, she was blamed. Misty had planned to stay at her Dad's house.

Misty had been close to Vera. The women had been friends since Heather was a toddler. Heather's death had devastated Vera. She and Misty had remained in touch, but Misty had noticed that Vera wasn't the same person afterwards. Misty turned on the radio and prayed that her friend would be all right.

Three hours later, Misty pulled of the expressway in search of a gas station. She found one in Saint Joseph, MI. After she parked, Misty opened the car door. The warmth of the bright sun made her feel better about the journey. Misty went in to find a bathroom, paid for her fuel, and went out. After she fueled her car and made it back to the freeway, Misty checked the time and realized that she was only an hour and a half away from Detroit.

When Misty saw the Southfield Expressway interchange, she took it. Misty rode until she saw Exit 9 and came up. She made a left turn onto Joy Road and drove down to Evergreen. She was starving and hunted for a Coney Island. The restaurant served everything on the menu twenty-four hours a day. Misty pulled around into the Drive -thru and ordered the All-American special and a small coffee.

She had just paid for and received her order when her cell phone rang. Misty bundled the plastic bag and juggled the coffee through the window. When she had her tray situated on the front seat, she searched through her purse to find the phone. She found it and looked at the screen. Vera had called. Misty pulled over and thought about the last time she'd seen Vera right after Heather's death. Misty had driven straight through to be by her side and when she'd called her then, she gotten a little more than what she wanted.

Chapter 4

"Hello" Vera said.

"Hey girl. Did you eat yet?" Misty said.

"I can't. My nerves are a wreck. I haven't been able to sleep."

"I'm on my way to pick you up so we can get something's done."

"Alright."

"See you in a minute."

Misty sighed and hoped that she could find the words of encouragement. She didn't know what to say to Vera any more now than she did at the hospital. Vera had turned to Misty for advice. Misty had given her honest opinion based on what she'd heard, but still urged her to speak with her grandmother before she made any decisions. Heather had suffered a stroke. The doctors had told them that they had done all they could do for her.

When Misty pulled up to the house in Highland Park, she wondered if she was in the right place. Trash piled high in the yard, broken toys and bottles littered the walkway. Misty reached for her cell phone to call Vera to be sure she was in the right place. Her eyes never left what appeared to be a long abandoned property.

Misty saw a filthy, torn sheet that partially covered a front window move to the side. Vera opened the door and stepped out on the porch, waving her arms in the air. Misty turned the car off and got out to go in. A she made to the front door, she tried to smile.

Misty clutched at her throat as soon as she stepped inside. The smell of rotted garbage and feces had made her gag. A lonely couch sat without cushions on a far wall. As far as Misty could see there was a foot deep layer of trash, left-over food, dirty clothes, and various alcohol bottles.

Vera reached out to hug Misty. Reluctantly, Misty hugged her. The odor of the house had sunk into her clothes and hair. Misty patted Vera's back and fought back tears. Another woman waded through the trash-covered mess and waved weakly. Vera sniffed and led Misty back out onto the porch by her hand.

"Do you have a cigarette?" Vera asked.

"They're in the car. Come on girl." Misty said.

When the women got in car and the door closed, Misty reached in her purse and pulled out a pack of Newport's. She watched as Vera rubbed her hands expectantly. When at last Vera was able to get one lit and puffed it, she exhaled and started to cough.

"What's going on here Vera? Do you mind if I help you straighten up or something after I stop by my Dad's house?"

"No, umm I got it."

"What about the other chick in there. She looked stoned out her mind. Is that your friend?"

"Oh that's Felicia. She lived upstairs but she got evicted. She has five kids and nowhere to go. Those twins of hers are a hot mess though. She smoked up her rent money. I kind of felt bad for her kids and she looked out for my kids when I was going through this stuff. There's nothing to me and her, she was just down and out for minute."

"That's so kind of you to be looking out for someone else at a time like this. I figured that maybe you had found you somebody."

"She ain't nothing to me. There ain't nothing pretty about her but her lips. All she does is lay on that filthy, pissy couch until late at night. Then she gets dressed and hits the streets."

"Oh and you're hanging out with her, at a time like this?"

"Yeah, I don't care about what she does. It's not my woman."

Misty said nothing as she put her key in the ignition and turned it on. The raggedy structure loomed like a house of untold horrors in the rearview mirror as she peeled away from the curb.

When Misty pulled up to the flat on Vinewood, she smiled when she saw her father sitting on the porch. He stood up, stretched, and sat a plastic cup on the porch railing. James came down the steps to his daughter. Misty put the car in park, jumped out, and rushed into father's arms.

The two hugged in the middle of the street for several minutes. It had been three months since he had laid eyes on her. Although James had helped his daughter move to Illinois, he had never liked the idea of her living four hours way. Every time he'd seen her, it brought a relief to his heart to know that she was okay.

Misty shut the car door and waited while her dad took her suitcase from the back seat. When Vera got out and spoke to James, he paused.

"Well, how in the hell are you?" James said.

"I'm good Pops, how are you?" Vera said.

Vera walked around the vehicle and reached out. He embraced her with his free hand and put his arm around her shoulder. The pair headed for the front door with Misty trailing close behind. When they arrived at the door, Misty realized she forgotten to lock her car. Nature was calling her and she asked Vera if she wouldn't mind locking up the car for her. Vera agreed and left.

Misty bolted for the bathroom. When she returned Vera was still outside. Misty thought it was curious but said nothing. Instead she walked up the window and looked out. .She saw Vera in the back seat of her car. James called to Misty from the kitchen and slowly she walked away. With a slight frown she went to go see what her dad wanted.

"I just had breakfast, but its some grits, fat back, and biscuits left. I can heat it up for you if you want." James said.

"Thanks dad, but I bought food I haven't even eaten yet."

"Ask Vera is she hungry? I can put it for later. I'd rather somebody eat this here. I don't like to waste no food."

"I'll go see."

When Misty went to go find her, Vera stepped through the door. Vera had her head down. It seemed that she avoided eye contact with both James and Misty. Misty looked surprised when Vera brushed past her asked for the bathroom. Misty assumed that she needed to use the restroom and shrugged.

"Do you want something to eat yet Vera?" Misty yelled through the door.

"Not yet." Vera replied.

A few moments later a puffy-faced Vera emerged from the bathroom.

"Are you okay?" James asked.

Vera burst into tears. Misty and James raced to her side to comfort her. They gently led a faltering Vera to the couch. She wailed openly and James handed Vera his handkerchief.

"My baby, oh God my child." Vera said.

Chapter 5

Vera and Misty had been friends and then some for a long time. Misty felt bad for Vera and her children. The tragedy was unusual but the situation wasn't. Vera had married young and quickly given birth to four children in rapid succession. Vera had told Misty her side of things.

Her husband was a promising street hustler, When they married they were good. Before long, he went from being the man to a client. The pressure of providing for children and habits became too much. Between the streets and lack of options, something had to give.

Misty didn't know how truthful Vera was about it and didn't care. It pained her to see the children lose. It appeared to Misty that the absences of a father figure and lack of long-term goals. The proverbial "live for today" syndrome that plagued many urban families had been at Vera's door too.

Misty thought herself very fortunate even without the presence of her children's father in their lives. James, Thomas, her uncles, and even her friend's husband, had stepped in and collectively supported her in the raising of her children. Vera's uncle B had done what he could to help her. However, Vera was strong-willed and Misty had a tendency to let the men handle men things.

Vera was a high-school drop out and self-described troubled child. She often thumbed her own nose at the rules. Every parent passes on what they've to give. In spite of that, Vera was a sweet generous person that loved her children.

Vera had one son. In sharp contrast to Thomas, Vera's boy had skills and talent that weren't groomed. The wiry, thin-framed boy had a gift of gab and basketball. Misty could see he had the skills to become a basketball legend, coach, sports announcer, or anything else he'd desired. While Vera had access to a support system, there was a hiccup in the ability to put it in place for the children.

Vera had suffered from depression. Her struggles eventually lead her to have a nightly drink. She was able to work and maintain but the stress had begun to show. Vera had come to depend on her brother Gio and his common-law wife, Aramis to help her care for the children often. It was such a night that tragedy struck.

Gio had stubborn streak of his own. He covered for the misdeeds of his nephew at times. The children left in their care didn't have to keep on chores, homework, or hygiene. The lack of structure quickly turned to chaos in Vera's absence. Gio took no responsibility and threw his sister in front of the train when all hell broke loose.

Aramis claimed that she'd cared for the Heather as if she were her own. When Heather became ill the first time, she dropped her off at the local hospital and left her there. Gio and Aramis often fought and argued viciously. After Heather's return, they fought again. Aramis left. Later ,when she heard that Heather had passed, someone called protective services and reported Vera for it.

Thomas was on the other side of town, up at dawn as he made rounds to pick up students. He was aware that some of his students missed class because the parents had a hard time financially for transportation. Although he'd hadn't missed school because for that reason, Thomas didn't care for school very much at first himself. Things changed when he found his reason to be there.

Once Thomas was on the lot, he began his drill and strength training with the kids. It warmed his heart to see the eagerness in those that wanted something better. Thomas had barely missed being just another soul that was lost on the Boulevard of Broken Dreams himself.

His parents and community had refused to let go. Detroit residents had become pissed off with the policies that presented their young men one of two choices. Get in the game and go to jail or hell for it. Those who had managed to escape the trap had formed their own safety net of love and support for the sake of the children.

After testing out of high school and his completion of college, Thomas had missed the bullet of being a just another black face in a sea of despair. He found a position as teacher's aid in the music department with his mentor. Mr. Base looked for the kids who had nothing. Gender didn't matter, he grew up in slums and could see a lack of direction hidden behind their eyes. He'd become part of the net that had been there for him.

He swiftly honed in and reached in. Sometimes it was through his own-shared story and other times it was as a concerned teacher and father figure. Whatever it was he could do he did, which included going in his pocket to feed them. Thomas didn't care for the recognition. He genuinely cared that he'd seen as many urban babies make it as possible.

James quietly beamed with pride. The price of that drum set had become immeasurable for him. James had struggled through the start of his life. To see his boy grow into a man brought a sense of good things to come for him and the future. James could clearly see, he team was going to win.

Misty wasn't that keen on the thought of being stuck with someone else's children, but admired her brother and father for doing so. James had a tendency to take those who preferred to skip school under his wings. James was a skilled mechanic as well. He'd show them how to fix things. Like James, Thomas had developed a just do it kind of attitude.

Misty liked to coddle children, love them up some, and send them on their merry way. Until she met Vera, that is. Vera's children had somehow managed to worm their way into her heart. They visited often and the two sets of children had melded into one. Misty woke up one day and realized that she had become mother to a brood of seven.

Although Misty was somewhat of a co-parent to Vera's children in their younger years, her, and Vera's relationship was strained. Misty believed that the children suffered from the tension between them. Misty hadn't seen Heather in more than a month prior to the funeral. Misty partially blamed herself for Heathers' death. As she looked into the casket that held Heather's body, it was a brutal slap in the face. She felt as though death had waltzed in a caught her asleep at her station.

The reality was there was little that Misty could have done. She didn't have any legal rights to the children. Her input had always been limited to what she knew and how accurate that information might be. Even though Misty understood her role in their lives was temporary, the knowledge didn't lessen the intense pain.

It was at that moment that she'd finally understood why Thomas did what he did. Misty hadn't thought about the sense of deep sense of loss that him or James must have felt when things turned out tragically. Her ex-husband and many other problems that she'd faced became pebbles compared to death. She pushed forward and hoped she had

j

Whether Thomas and James knew, Misty refused to marry again, because she hadn't seen the likes of a mate quite like either one of them. She thought earnestly in her heart that Vera's children would've had a different sense of the world had they been a closer part of her family. So much so that she'd been careful to allow her own children to be around them both as much as possible. The men lives were closely tied to a structure of strength that Misty marveled at.

Chapter 6

Misty was at a lost for word once again. It shredded her heart to feel so helpless while Vera went through something that she could only witness. The situation had careened out of control so fast. Misty did her best to remain close by and block out the sound of Vera's misery.

Misty was grateful when she heard the sound of her cell phone ringing. She looked around for where she had put purse, when her dad pointed at the coffee table. Misty slowly went and ruffled through her bag. She answered on the third ring.

"What's up doe?" Misty said.

"Hey baby, this your big brother. I heard you were swinging through. You make it yet?" Thomas said.

"Yeah, I'm here. I'm going to stay for a few days. I might go east in a while though."

"Okay, glad you made it in safe. I love you."

"Love you too."

Misty hung up and turned her attention back to Vera and James.

"I'm going to leave you two to catch up and go have a sip of beer outside." James said.

"Okay dad." Misty said.

Misty went over to the couch and sat next to Vera. She wrapped her arm around her friend and hugged her tightly. Vera blew her nose and the fabric and her body shivered. Misty waited for Vera to say something. At last, Vera spoke.

"I can't believe these people want to see me do jail time for Heather's death. It wasn't like I was negligent. I've taken care of my kids. I always left them with people I trusted. She's been hypoglycemic since she was four. I've always done what they told me. She didn't live to be fifteen years old and I just said fuck it, you know?"

"Well, at this point we just have to move forward. I hope that everything works out for you."

"You don't understand. I think that they are going to convict me."

"Why do you think that? They still haven't heard your side."

"They aren't trying to hear my side. Someone called protective Services on me before they had even pronounced my baby gone."

"Did you ever find out who did or why?"

"Only what was said by the worker. I told you all that."

"That still sounds like someone close to you. What I don't understand is why anyone would wait until it was too late to help her before they called protective services. It would seem that if you were that bad of a mother, those concerned citizens would have called before now."

"I don't know. I suspect it was some of those old dusty hood-rats from the block."

"I hope not, it one thing to not like you. It's a whole different picture to kick someone when they are already down. She was the baby. My guts say that there is more to this than what has been said."

"Some days this feels like a bad dream, I keep waiting on Heather to run inside and hug my neck and ask me for candy or something."

Vera lean back onto the couch and rested her head on the wall. Less than forty-eight hours away she would have to stand in front of a judge. The thought chilled her to the core. Vera pursed her lips and sighed.

Misty's cell phone rang again. When she went to answer it, she realized it was someone from Vera house. She passed her the phone and rubbed her arms gently while Vera answered. Misty peered out of the window while Vera talked.

"What the fuck you mean where I'm at. You're my child and everything those stupid bitches tell you to do you do it. I don't have a reason to run off and I don't have to tell you every time I decide to get some damn air." Vera said.

Vera wiped her eyes as a fresh batch of tears had begun to roll. She touched Misty's shoulder with the cell phone. Misty took her phone and laid it down on the table. Misty reached over and grasped her hand and squeezed it.

"Hang in there kiddo." Misty said.

"People can be so selfish. I lost my child and I'm about to lose my freedom. My own kids won't even ask me how I'm doing; instead they call me up asking for money. I'm not watching no kids or nothing else. I'm going to spend the last few days of my freedom doing what I want to do." Vera said.

"Do you girl." Misty said.

"I knew you'd understand. I'm glad you came."

"I don't understand anything but I wouldn't wish this on my worst enemy."

A few hours later Vera asked to be taken back home. Misty grabbed her car keys and the women headed off to Highland Park. James had prepared dinner and Misty was anxious to get back there. The collard greens and fried chicken smell had settled into their clothes. On the way to drop Vera off, Misty felt her stomach growl in anticipation of her father's food.

Misty had dropped Vera off and made it back to her father's place. When she walked in, James was already setting the table. Misty kissed her father on the cheek and went to wash her hands. After she was done, Misty stepped quickly to have a seat at the table.

"Thanks dad. I've been eating out of restaurants for the past three months." Misty said.

"Why, your mother taught you how to cook." James asked.

"Just laziness dad, I get so tired of cooking for one that I resorted to picking up food instead."

"Are you and Vera going to work something out?"

"I hadn't thought about it. So what have you been up to?"

"Oh well after we eat I'd planned to catch this movie on THIS. I think "Seven Brides for Seven Brothers" will be on tonight. You really think they gone send her to jail?"

"I don't know dad."

"Did you touch base with you're brother since you've been here?"

"Yeah dad."

Chapter 7

The morning of the first interview, Vera called Misty before daylight. Apprehension and fear filled Misty for her friend. Misty knew that she should be prepared to offer words of encouragement but none came to mind. She answered the phone, just the same.

"My lawyer is an idiot and he's not doing anything to help me." Vera wailed.

"Ok, try to call down." Misty said.

"I'm going to call Mrs. Joyce and Mrs. Helen and ask them to pray for your safe return back to life."

"I appreciate that. Listen Misty…"

"Yes, I don't want you to go in with me."

"Why not?"

"If they take me jail, I don't want you have to watch that. I just called to say thank you."

"I will respect your wishes, so know I'm there with you in spirit."

"Yeah me too."

The day seemed to drag on as Misty awaited word from Vera. It was nearly eight in the evening when she'd given up hope. Misty felt her heart breaking for Vera and her family. The double tragedy of their remaining children to have lost their mother would be hard to swallow.

Misty finally willed herself to get her bag and leave. James had a lady friend coming for the evening and Misty wanted to be gone when his company arrived. Her father had been supportive the past two days and she thought he deserved to have his house back to enjoy his company. She'd planned to stop and see her brother before she pulled out.

Misty found James sitting on the porch with a beer in hand. She kissed her dad on the forehead and told him she was leaving. James walked his daughter to the car. He cautioned her about driving too fast and told her to have a safe trip as she pulled off.

"I got to run to the east and touch base with a few people over there and then hit the road. It will be late before I get in, but I'll call you."

"Ok, take care."

Misty pulled back into traffic looked for the Mid-town Cash and Go store and turned down Alger. It wasn't long before Nelia came out to the car screaming. Misty smiled and clapped her hands together. Misty slid out from the car and ran to hug her sister.

"Hey hoe, look at you looking all Hollywood and shit." Misty said.

"You know Earl was asking about you. He said he saw a picture of you from the last time you was here." Nelia said.

"What did he say?"

"That you looked exactly the same as he remembered you."

"Oh. That's nice."

Nelia playfully hit at Misty. Misty giggled and turned her head. He was one of the cutest guys she'd known growing- up. Her sister was kind of gossipy, but was quite the match-maker. Misty knew that she was headed back out of town and wasn't going to look him up. She grasped her sisters' hand and they went into her house.

Nelia oldest daughter, Leticia ran up and hugged Misty. She knew that her Aunt Misty kept candy in her purse and she was quite the little schemer. Misty reached down in her bag and grabbed a handful of peppermints and handed them to her.

Nelia's and her husband Bill had bought a large house and worked hard to build into the home of their dreams. It was heartwarming to see him moving throughout the house tending to his daughters. The scene uplifted Misty's soul in the midst of everything else. The house had seemed to blossom into a multi- level palace of luxury.

"Hi Bill" Misty said.

"Hey Misty" Bill answered.

"The yard looks wonderful."

"Thanks"

Nelia grabbed Misty's hand and led her through the house. She pointed out some updates that the couple had made. The women ended up in the kitchen. Bill left the room and Nelia leaned in close to her sister's ear.

"I think he's seeing someone else. Girl he's been fixing up this house like you wouldn't believe." Nelia said.

"Maybe he's just being a good husband. It appears to me that he loves you and the children very much." Misty said.

"You were married five minutes. You know what it looks like ain't always what it is."

"Why do you think he's cheating, just because he's fixing up the house?"

"No, but yes, before we bumped into Kemp at the gas station on Livernois, I could barely get him to take out the trash."

"His cousin Kemp?"

"Yeah, girl, he looked nervous and Kemp went out of her way to speak to him. She had this little twitch in her neck almost as if she dared him not to speak back."

"So that doesn't mean anything."

"It does when her male co-worker kept hitting on my husband openly at that barbecue."

"Oooooh, I don't think that he'd do that to you and the girls."

"Something got him cleaning, building, and some other stuff like you wouldn't believe."

"Yeah, he probably don't want that kind of attention. He might have decided that that was cue to re-invest in you and the girls. Is Baby Sister coming here this year or are you guys going over to Ohio?"

"I don't know yet."

Nelia's house phone made a shrill chirp. The phone hung on the wall near the doorway. When Nelia picked it up she turned away from Misty to talk. Misty looked around, then she felt a tug on her arm. Leticia had returned and had her little hand opened for more candy.

"Where are your sisters?" Misty asked.

"They went to an after school program. I didn't have to go 'cause it's for babies. I'm a big girl."

Misty reached in her purse and gave her two more peppermints. Nelia hung up the phone. She gave her best smile but the creases in her brow made her appear worried. She reached up and ran her hand through her hair.

"That was Thomas, he's on his way over here in a while." Nelia Said.

"Okay, I'm going to go out and make a few runs before he gets here." Misty said.

She was anxious to see him and get on the road. By the time Misty got in her car and lit a cigarette, she heard music coming from down the block. A large shiny Cadillac Escalade rolled up behind her car. Misty felt the vibrations of the sound system from inside of her car.

Chapter 8

Thomas, parked his truck and turned of the ignition. Misty chuckled when she saw him get out of the car. He was dressed impeccably in a black suit and crisp white shirt. Since they'd been children, Thomas had been one of the neatest guys Misty had known. Her closed his vehicle door and walked up to Misty's car.

"Where my hug?" Thomas said.

"With you're sugar." Misty said.

"Well then lay it on me."

Thomas opened the car door for his sister. Misty stepped out and hugged and kissed his cheek. When Thomas grinned, Misty couldn't help but smile too. She brushed at her clothes and stood back while her brother looked her over. Thomas closed the car door and leaned his massive frame on it.

"So, you didn't think to mention that you were leaving state huh?" Thomas asked.

"I know and I apologize. I just woke up one morning and decided to pack and go." Misty said.

"Un huh. Where are the kids?"

"I took them with me the first time. They stayed with me until everyone was grown. When I came back, they stayed. They decided they didn't care for a quiet life or anything about me for that matter. So, since it's just me, I left. Thanks to all the help I had with them, I figured they'd be alright."

"What do you mean the seem not care for you? You're their mother."

"Well, they decided that they would rather be around their dad. I'd served my purpose and was basically useless to them. Once the oldest one put it in perspective for me, I accepted their positions and kept it moving."

"Put what in perspective for you? You stayed and he left?"

"I know, I gave them what I could. They got grown and decided it wasn't good enough. I had to be the person to check and correct them their whole lives and in return, they've made it plain to me and everyone that would listen how much they hate me for it. He got to be the good one for everything he didn't do and I became the villain for staying. Hell, by the time they were through, I was the worst thing that had ever happened to them. So it is was it is."

"You're kidding right?"

"No. The oldest one said I was never his mother and that Mama had raised him, I never taught him anything, and I spent my life pawning them off on other people other people and raising other people's kids. The girl runs around calling any woman she sees Mama, and the youngest said being around me made him miserable and depressed. Once they got with their dad and had a family conference, they had the oldest one represent the four of them as a family minus me. The bottom line is they wished I would die and hopefully bitter and alone with no one to love me. On top of that, I was informed that I needed to check myself into a mental institution for being a woman in the first place."

"Do they know what really happened or are they…?"

"No Thomas they don't and please don't tell them if you see them. They've decided the want nothing to with me. Leave it just like that. I'll always be their mother and I'll always love them but after a lifetime of abuse and mistreatment, maybe this is God's way of solving it."

"So, you walked away. But I'm your family too. You can't let no kids run you."

"That's just it, they didn't run me. They told me to make a choice. Die with them or live without them. I chose life. As long as they are determined to run into the pain what could I do? These aren't little kids, these are grown people that I'm confident have common sense. Once they decided they didn't believe in God or a higher power, I was done. I'm not perfect, no one is. That's something you strive for daily. To be a better person than you were the day before. However, It wasn't their business. I didn't want to his slave. I can't love or care for someone that thinks my place is behind them or beneath their boot. After he explained that I was to cook, clean, and perform my wifely duties, which he clarified as have sex with him whenever he said so, I ran. He brought other women into our bed. He offered me to other people like I was an extra seat in the house. He was angry that I wouldn't work two jobs to take of him and that I wanted to get an education. Once he started lying on the kids and hurting them too, I did what I thought a mother should do. The main one that's championing his destruction and treating me the worse is the one he tried to kill first. When I saw a grown man take my baby and hold him upside down and beat him like a savage dog for asking for food, I wanted to kill him. That was the moment that I realized that I could either take my babies and run or end up spending my life in prison and never see them again. He's a convincing liar and he immediately started using law agencies to abuse me too. He's tried to kill me and them twice. Both times, God intervened. I don't know what lies ahead but I don't believe he's brought me this far to leave me, The funny thing is, I'm not bitter or alone. I never was and I never will be. I got to see them grown. I've protected them as long as I could. When I realized that he'd been using them to keep tabs on me and continually bring misery into my life, it was time to go. I'm not the first woman in the world to not see her children or grandbabies. I hope I'm the last though. I took some of my free time and wrote a few books to keep myself busy. Might write a few more. Mama said if you don't stand for something, you'll fall for anything. "

"So you're going to keep in touch right? You're not going back down there and never come back are you?"

"They told him where I was again. So, I won't be going there for long. My number will still be the same, but I can't trust them. I won't go any farther than to say, I'll let you know that I'm okay."

"I'm your family, I didn't do anything to you, why can't you tell me?"

"I don't think you'd tell him or them, but it makes me feel better this way. You can't tell what you don't know. I just came to show some love to the family and dip. That's enough about me and my life. How are you? It's good to see you."

"I'm blessed, It's good to see you too sis. I'm sorry that your going through so much. I'll keep you in my prayers but then I always have. I've gone through a lot myself, but like you God intervened. Maybe not when I wanted him, but always right on time. He's going to fix this too, just keep the faith."

"I never lost it."

Misty hugged her brother once more. She waited while he opened her car door and she slid into the driver seat. She watched as Thomas nodded while she buckled in, before he walked into the house to see Nelia. Misty started her car and pulled away from the curb just as Thomas opened the door to the house.

Chapter 9

Vera woke up at four a.m. She rubbed her shoulders to ward off the sense of dread that she felt. A light sheen of moisture covered her skin. Her stomach churned every time she thought at about the cold prison cell that may have been prepared for her. She scooted to the edge of the bed, before she finally stood up and stretched.

There was a short checklist of things she wanted to do, before her ride came to pick her up for the second interview. Vera had decided she didn't want any long drawn out good-byes, if she was arrested. She had made peace with the fact that today that she might be taken in.

From the very the start Vera was confused when Protective Services had claimed they had tried to contact her. Later, she would find that her brother and his girlfriend had known all along. When her brother Gio had spoken with the worker, he's literally thrown his sister under the bus. By the time Vera spoke to the Investigator, the woman was already biased.

She remembered clearly how humiliated the woman had made her feel. Vera had risen early the morning after Heather passed. Sleep had never come to ease her mind, in the hours that she lay on the couch. Before she could take care of the first order of business, the drama had started.

Vera sat up on the couch and waited until the funeral home was open. The most difficult task that she faced on that day was to call the funeral home and make arrangements for Heather. Minutes had begun to seem like hours as she waited in the dark and past the risen sun for the business to open.

She had laid the card right next to the phone on the coffee table. It had been given to her at the hospital when the funeral home had to come to pick up Heather. Vera had to strengthen herself to get ready to speak with someone about how she wanted to have her child buried. Every atom of her body rebelled at the thought. Her hands quivered as she picked up the phone from the cradle and started to dial the numbers. Vera breathed deeply as she put the receiver to her ear and listened.

"Good morning, how can I help you?" The receptionist answered.

"Hello, this is Vera Black. I'm calling to set up an appointment to make arrangement for my daughter, Heather Black." Vera said.

"I'm sorry for your loss, could you please hold while I check to see who is available?"

"Yeah."

Music began to play while Vera held the phone. Minutes ticked by while she waited for someone to pick up. The frustration grew after five minutes had passed and still no one had come back to the line. Agitated, Vera hung up and dialed the funeral home again.

The phone rang several times but no one answered. Vera grew frantic that her child was there and no one would speak to her. She slammed down the phone and decided to go there instead. Before she could get up the phone rang.

"Hello?" Vera said.

"Hello, this is Director Benson of OH Funeral Services. Is Vera Black in?"

"This is she."

"I understand that you called this morning to make arrangements for Heather. I'm sorry to have kept you on hold but the police were here."

"Okay so what? The lady could have just told me that and I would have called back later. I just want to make an appointment. The police being there don't have anything to do with me or my daughter."

"I'm afraid that it does. I have just been told that we can't have any services for Heather until you speak to Protective Services."

"What?"

"I'm sorry ma'am, but until you speak with an Investigator, we can't bury your daughter. They came in first thing this morning to inform us that they were looking for you. They left a number for you to call. If you choose to show up here, we have been instructed to call the police. I can't do anything for you while waiting for this to be cleared up."

Vera slammed the phone receiver down. A new wave of hurt had overwhelmed her. She covered her face in her hands. The sound of the Director's voice boomed in her mind.

"Why me? I did nothing wrong. I can't believe this shit. My baby is gone and the state is holding her hostage? This ain't right. I was at two different hospitals with her. If they thought I did something wrong why in the hell didn't they say something then?" She cried.

Vera used her fingers to wipe her eyes. She then rubbed her temples against the pain that had begun to thump there. It had been more than forty-eight hours since she had last eaten or bathed. Her stomach growled and she put her hands on the couch to steady herself. After several attempts to get up, at last her legs steadied enough for her to stand on.

Chapter 10

It was nearly eleven a.m. before Misty had arrived at Vera' house. When she pulled up, Misty prayed that she would be able to be a source of strength. Vera had called her and she was extremely upset. Misty had taken her to the first interview and had only heard a portion of what she said.

When Vera came to the car, Misty gasped at the sight of the woman's face. Her eyes were sunken sockets of pure misery. A glassy coat of water covered the lenses. Vera looked as if she'd aged twenty years in two days.

"Good morning, let's get this over with." Vera said wearily

"Hey girl" Misty said.

"Hey"

"How are your other children doing?"

"As okay as they can be."

Vera was usually open and talkative. It came as no shock to Misty that she was subdued and quiet. The creases in her forehead along with dark rings around her eyes made Vera looked as if she'd been out at a party all night. Her clothes were wrinkled and she'd put on her tennis shoes with no socks. At the moment Vera appeared to in need of a long stint in a rehabilitation facility.

Misty had been to the center where Vera had to report. She drove to the 1-75 entrance, merged into traffic and went to the building. When they arrived, Misty pulled into a parking spot and began to rifle through her compact disc collection. Vera sighed loudly as she opened the door.

Two minutes had passed and so far Vera had only managed to put one foot on the ground. She fumbled with her shirt and brushed at her hair with her hand. Misty sense that Vera was terrified to go in. Finally, Vera got out of the car and stood with the door opened. Nervously she looked around and ducked her head back down inside the car.

"Misty, would you mind coming with me? I don't know what's up with these people." Vera said.

"Okay." Misty said.

When Misty turned off the engine and got out of the car, she saw the relief on Vera face. She walked around the car and put her hand on her shoulder.

"It's going to be alright." Misty said.

Vera didn't respond, but stepped back to let Misty go in first. The women went into the Protective Services Headquarters. As soon as they entered the door they were greeted by a female security officer. The officer asked Misty for her identification and the reason of her visit. Misty.

Misty told the guard that she was there with Vera. She reached into her purse and pulled out her driver's license and handed it to the guard. The guard took the card and looked at it then looked up and studied Misty's face. Satisfied that Misty was the person on the card, the guard asked Vera for her identification, she passed Misty her license back.

"I'm Vera Black, all I have is my Medicaid Card on me. I didn't know think to bring any ID." Vera said.

"Then how am I supposed to know you are who you say you are then?" The officer asked.

"You don't, but I doubt many people come in here and claim to be anything. Look, I don't want to be here as is. My baby just died and I don't have for your shit right now."

"I'm sorry for your loss, but you still have to talk like you have some sense. I can tell you right now that attitude will piss a worker off. let me check to see who has your case Ms. Black. Please wait have a seat over there."

The guard pointed to a row of chairs along the wall. They women walked over and took a seat while the guard typed data into her computer. A moment later she picked up the phone and dialed someone. When she hung up, she informed the women that the worker would be out in a few minutes.

Ten minutes later, an African-American woman with thinning dreadlocks came to the main door. The waiting room was empty except for Vera and Misty. The woman held a manila file in her hand. The woman surveyed the room before she called Vera's name.

Vera stood up and walked to the door before she greeted the woman. Misty had decided that this was good time to go out and have a cigarette. When she got up and headed for the door she heard the worker call her by her last name.

"Excuse me, Mrs. Jordan; I need to speak with both of you."

Chapter 11

The hair on the back of Misty's neck stood up. She turned and walked towards the door where Vera and the woman were standing. Misty scowled as she approached them. She wondered how the woman had known her last name.

The worker instructed them to follow her into an interview room. When they were all inside, the worker closed the door and offered them a seat. When the worker sat on the opposite side of the table and opened the folder, Misty could partially see the report.

"Hi, I'm Jolie Hurlbut. I'm the worker that's been assigned to your case. I'm glad you came down to talk to me. I've been trying to reach you for three days and I had begun to worry that you didn't have any interest in talking with me Vera." Mrs. Hurlbut said.

"I don't." Vera replied.

"Ms. Black, with all due respect, you child is dead. I want to know what happened."

"For that you stopped her funeral?"

"I'm very concerned about you and your family."

"What the hell do want to ask me? If you were so concerned with me and my family this could have waited. Talking isn't going to bring my child back."

"Look here, I'm the law. I can write up a report that will have you thrown in jail right now. I've spoken to your sister-in-law. I know all about what kind of person you really are."

"If you listened to that bitch then you're stupid."

"Why don't you tell me your side then?"

"Excuse me..." Misty said.

The worker turned her nose up at Misty and huffed. Misty had been able to foresee that a storm was brewing between the women. She'd interjected to calm the situation if possible. The worker crossed her arms defiantly.

"Yeah." Mrs. Hurlbut said.

"How do you know my name and why am I here?" Misty asked.

"Let me see, are you the mother of Tasha, Jamie, and Cornell Simpson."

"Yes I am, however you still haven't answered my question. Why do you care?"

"Well your name and the name of your children are included in the report."

"What do you mean included?" Misty asked.

Mrs. Hurlbut shuffled through the papers in front of her. She started to read the list of alleged complaints lodged against Vera. The worker had barely made it the fourth sentence when she recited Misty's and her children's full names, dates of birth, phone numbers, and address. Misty waited while the worker finished.

"Ms. Jordan are you and Vera lovers, life partners or whatever you call yourselves these days?" Mrs. Hurlbut asked.

"My personal relationship past or present is none of your business. I don't understand what anyone's sexual identity has to do with a child that has passed." Misty said.

"The question was quite simple, are you her lover? I can expand my investigation to include you and your children, her daughters, and anyone else I chose to. I suggest that you answer my question."

"I'm have no intention of responding to inquiries about whether my relationship with Ms. Black has ever been sexual. That would be the same as me asking if you gave your man oral sex before work this morning. It has nothing to do with your purpose. She needed a ride to get here, so I brought her. Nevertheless, who I let in my panties isn't a matter that Protective Services needs to concern themselves with. I prefer older partners so there's no children involved."

"I take that denial as a yes then."

"Take it how you want, but from the tone of what you just read, whoever called you seemed to be more concerned with her relationship with me than the welfare of her children. To me that sounds like someone that's mad that maybe she didn't come to them when they called."

"I'm not at liberty to say who called."

"You don't have to. You have too much personal information about me, for it be a neighbor or distance admirer."

"Why do you say that Ms. Jordan?"

"Vera and I don't have the same friends. I'm rarely around her people and my children and her children barely see each other. Now, if you scarcely are seen with say one of your co-workers, yet an investigator had a report with excessive personal information about you, how long would your list of suspects be?"

"Very perceptive Ms. Jordan, I supposed it would be limited to people I work with or someone that hung out around us."

"Okay, now I flat out deny every lie in that report. I've no idea what did or didn't happen at that household. I didn't live there. Whenever Ms. Black was low of supplies to care for her children, she had no problem reaching out to ask for support from me or anyone else for that matter. Now if you'll excuse me, I'm going out to have a cigarette now."

Misty stood and walked to the door to leave.

"I'd appreciate it Mrs. Hurlbut that despite what you think of the Triangle type, that you will find it in your heart to call that funeral home and allow her to bury Heather. That baby's life was hard enough as it were. It's disgraceful to hold up her home-going services just to prove a point or out anyone. Please don't make her death any harder than it already is. Thank you and have a good day." Misty said.

"You too Ms. Jordan, I'm sure we'll be seeing each other again soon." Mrs. Hurlbut replied.

Fifteen minutes later an exhausted and teary eyed Vera emerged from the building. Misty lit a cigarette for her before the car door opened. Vera drug herself into the front seat. When she closed the vehicle door, Vera collapsed against the seat and screamed in anguish.

Big Body Base

Chapter 12

Misty pulled off and let Vera have her moment of grief. She felt deeply for her pain and had vowed to do whatever she could do to help Vera. When she pulled back up to the dilapidated house in Highland Park, Misty parked and waited while Vera pulled herself together.

"Before you go is there anything I can do?" Misty asked.

"I don't want to talk to these funeral home people no more. Do you think you could do that for me?" Vera asked.

"Sure."

Vera leaned over and touched Misty's cheek. Misty turned her head toward Vera with tears in her eyes. Vera leaned over and kissed Misty passionately. Misty found herself responding before she pulled away.

"Look I know you're under a bunch of pressure right now. If this is what's supposed to happen it will Vera, but right now we need to bury our daughter. Please let's just focus on our child." Misty said.

"I need you and when this is over, I'm going to figure out how to make this right. I don't know where to even start." Vera said.

"Let's start by you getting some rest and I'll go ahead and see what I can get done. I'll call you later."

When Vera got out of the car and closed the door, she walked up on the porch. Her hand hadn't touched the metal remnants, of what used to be a screen door, before it opened. Misty saw the same woman from earlier that day. She stood in the door-way half-dressed with a can of beer in her hand. Vera waved at Misty, then brushed past the woman and went inside.

Misty put the car in drive and pulled off. She drove down Woodward to the Davison entrance and made her way back to her dad's house. When she pulled up in front of her father's house, Misty sat there quietly for a moment before she went inside. She gently touched with her lips with her index finger then got out of the car.

James met her at the door. As soon as he opened it to let his daughter inside, she squealed with delight and hugged her dad's neck. The aroma of fresh homemade biscuits and bacon wafted through the air. He smiled at her and stepped to the side to let her in.

"I hope you haven't eaten yet. The food is almost ready. You still eat poached eggs right?" James asked.

"Yes daddy, I do. Haven't had any in a while though. That would mean I have to do it. My stove is so clean, it looks like it just came from the showroom." Misty replied.

"Well that's no good baby. You need to find yourself a mate or something. You ain't working up no appetite. I don't like you being alone no how. I'd like to know that somebody was there to look after my baby. With your mama gone, it feels like all I do is worry about my children. Seems I took up where she left off.

I remember when I use to come home from work. We'd sit up for a while and she filled me in on everything that was going on with y'all. That woman had her finger on the pulse of this family, like an emergency room doctor all the time. If something was going on with you, she had already figured out what to do before the problem ever came to be."

"I know dad, I miss her too."

"Yeah, that woman was one of a kind. Suppose I never will figure out how she got y'all to tell her shit that I would have never thought to ask you."

"It wasn't like that dad. You say it as if we kept secrets from you. Mama just had a way with people, not to say that you don't. She was something special though."

"Yeah, your right, even I told her things that I'd never tell another living soul. No doubt it went to heaven with her. I guess that why it warms my heart to see you. You look so much like her and sometimes you talk like her too. It sure would be nice to hear the pitter-patter of little feet running around here again though. You could have more kids."

"Daddy?"

"Yeah."

"Let it go."

"I'm just saying that's all."

"When I get done traveling, shopping, and enjoying myself, I might. The kids aren't babies any more. Let them have kids and whatnot. It's a lot of work, raising a family that is. I was blessed. I did what you asked of me, I married, had kids and raised them. If it hadn't of been for you and Mama, I don't know that it would have turned out as well as it did. Even Vera is catching hell and she was married first. Four babies later things didn't work out.

Her child needs to be buried, there's no insurance, the man rarely saw them babies and without the support of friends and family they might've been left to the gutter. I'm not judging either one of them but I don't want to push my luck. I'm done having kids."

James reached out and hugged his daughter tightly. He rested his chin on the top of her head. James desperately wanted to see a part of him that was innocent. He wanted to be assured that his legacy would continue in the future and for him that meant more grandbabies.

"Yeah, I understand. I just want you to know that if you decided to have a baby, the father could get the hell on right after we got what we needed. As soon as find someone to say I do, you can right back to I don't and that would be fine would with me."

"Daddy you're something else. As long you get a grandchild."

"I'm wise enough to know that a marriage and raising children is a lot of work. I see where you headed with that but fairytales don't always come true. From what I know about women they usually tend to want to forever with the baby's daddy. Yet and still it don't always turn out that way. No matter how much they plan it that way.

Some men are gone be there no matter what and some will talk like a man and run off faster than a girl when the pressure starts to get to them. Then again some of these women ain't fit to give birth to nothing either. I ever tell you about sea turtles? They come on shore, lay their eggs, cover it with sand, and swim right back out to sea. They don't even stick around long enough to see what the baby looks like. It's six of one and a half dozen of the other I suppose.

I remember a guy that married this woman and they had a few babies. He didn't want to work, play with his friends and cars all day like a kid, left her to catch the bus in the cold with those babies while he drove around. Then when she decided she had enough of his shit the best he could to for the mother of his children was drag her name through the mud. He walked up to me as bold as can be one day as said that he'd just caught her in the bed with another woman.

I laughed at him and told him that if I came home and found my wife in the bed with another woman, I'd keep my mouth shut and see if they needed any help. That's what I mean though, he can talk the talk but when it's time to step up that can be a different story. He'd moved into her house as it were. After she found out he was running around telling her business like a gossipy old biddy, she left him and got her another place. The minute he found out where it was, he burnt it down to the ground. That spiteful son of a bitch did it right at Christmas time too.

Left his own wife and children homeless without so much as a bath rag to wash her behind. He refused to help her or the kids. It wasn't long before she got back on her feet. He met some new woman and moved into her house the same way he did the first wife. That's when the first girl came out and said that she wasn't the first woman he'd done that to. In fact that the bastard had knocked up a girl on Hamilton, right before he'd run off and married the woman whose house he'd burned down."

James let his daughter go and walked over to the window and looked out. Misty saw her dad take his handkerchief from his back pocket and wipe near his eyes. He didn't look back at his daughter as she went to bathroom to wash her hands so she could go eat.

James shook his head and prayed once again that his daughter would understand his desire to see her with a mate.

Chapter 13

Misty and her dad had shared their meal quietly. After they were done she cleared the table and did the dishes. With a heavy heart she sat down on the couch and picked up the house phone to call the funeral home. Misty stomach was full of food yet her heart was full of grief.

After a series of phone calls, Misty had made arranged the appointments for Vera. She tried to call Vera to check on her and inform of the progress. The phone rand several time but went to voicemail. Misty hung up and decided to wait and try her again in a while.

Just then the phone rang. Misty answered it. She listened and clutched her hand to her throat. Tears formed in her eyes.

"Listen, you are about as stupid as they come. You keep calling her . She's in the bed with me and she's sleep. She don't need you or your help. I got this." A female said.

"Who is this?" Misty asked.

"She already told you who I was. Anyway just finish playing secretary, but don't be calling her just because you feel like it. It's me that she loves and she's been playing you the whole time. She only runs to you when she's mad at me."

"First off don't ever call this number again. Second of all I don't give two flying fucks about you and nothing about you. How stupid are you to embarrass yourself to call me? If that's your chick then why is she talking to me at all?"

"I let her do whatever she wants. That's how I keep her happy."

"Then let me tell you what makes her happy. Seeing me. Most of the time she just want's some to talk to You talking, when she's taking your money to travel to see me. Or did you think she needed to come to down there for car parts for real? Let me tell you something you ignorant little twit, when she with you, she's thinking about me ."

"You really think your hot shit don't you? I'm not going anywhere."

"I don't care if you do. You're the one that has to put up with nonsense. The minute she get's herself together, the second that this is all over with, watch where she ends up."

"Go to hell."

"No, I'm not. Think what you will about me, but you must be worried about something or you wouldn't be saying anything to me. "

"I don't know why you can't just leave her alone. All the stuff she's says about you, it looks stupid that you'd even reach out to her."

"Correction, she calls me. I don't know what she tells you, but that's what it is. She got you over there living in filth and grime. All those bad ass kids running around. As soon as she get's money she brings it to me. I wasn't trying to take her from you, if what she wants is a high-yellow hot mess, then girlfriend have at it. Just please take care of those kids, make that house a home, and teach them something that makes sense, like how to clean up for starters. You think I want her for a lover and it's not like that. Every person needs someone to talk to."

"You are one sorry excuse of a woman."

"I didn't call you, and you called here. Now you want to hear it? Here it goes. She's loves my stupid ass. When "your boo" needs a woman of substance, she comes to me. If you were so important then why didn't you make arrangements? Why would she call me at all? Trust and believe, I'm not out to hurt you're feeling. I have things in my own life to worry about. I don't know everything about her and I'm not going to say that you're lying. Still, change starts with me, not her. It's something about me as a person that attracts her. Maybe she believes that I can be of some help or comfort. Either way it's alright to try. If she's on some bullcrap, it'll come out. I don't need you to call me insulting or belittling me, you don't know me."

"She's taking you for a ride."

"Is that what you called to say."

"You're a whore."

"Is that what you called me for, to play elementary school games? Get the off of this phone with that. When she wakes up tell her I called."

"I wish I would."

"When she finds out I called and you interfered, she gone turn on you like a rabid dog. I want you see what it feels like when she jumps up and run past you to get to me."

"You a nasty hoe."

"Didn't she use you for a broom, when she dragged your ass down the hall by your leg, in front of your kids? I can assure you that I never took any ass whippings."

"That's not your business fool, where she at now? Lying in bed next to me, that's where! Y'all ain't got shit in common. The only reason she keeps running to me is because you give head and I don't."

"No doubt good orals skills are an asset. I'd give you some lessons, but I don't do pissy panties. While you on the phone with me, she needs to eat, get your lazy ass up and cook dinner and clean that house. You've been laying on those nasty sheets so long, they have your ass prints on them. She's over there because I'm not willing to live like that. Thank you for taking care of her for me though. I appreciate it. You've taken up as much of my time as I'm going to allow. Goodbye."

Misty heard the click as the line went dead. She chuckled aloud. One thing her mother had taught her was to never chase behind a lover. There are too many fish in the sea, to spend all day chasing one. Misty hadn't called back. Vera constantly called Misty though.

Misty hadn't wanted a relationship with Vera. She's been peeved that the female had verbally attacked her just the same. Misty had been through so much with Scott, Vera, and life that she just wanted some time to herself. Nevertheless, Misty was no longer in a position to have to put up with abuse from anyone and she didn't.

She went out and shopped for suitable clothing for her and all the children to wear for the funeral. The next day she'd attended the appointment with Vera and her cousin there for support. Less than a week later, the family was finally able to put little Heather to rest.

Misty stayed the day after the funeral and spent some time with the kids. When she pulled out from her fathers' house with a heavy heart she wondered how long before she came back. The long drive back gave her plenty of time to think. No charges had been filed on Vera and Misty had left.

Chapter 14

The day before the trial Vera had called Misty before daylight. Apprehension and fear filled Misty for her friend. Misty knew that she should be prepared to offer words of encouragement, but none came to mind. Vera wasn't aware that Misty was in Detroit yet.

She answered the phone, just the same.

"My lawyer is an idiot and he's not doing anything to help me." Vera wailed.

"Ok, try to call down." Misty said.

"I'm going to call Mrs. Joyce and Mrs. Helen and ask them to pray for your safe return back to life."

"I appreciate that. Listen Misty…"

"Yes, I don't want you to be there okay."

"Why not?"

"If they take me jail, I don't want you have to watch that. I just called to say thank you and I love you."

"I will respect your wishes, so know I'm there with you in spirit. I hope to hear from you this afternoon."

"Yeah me too."

She had planned to pull out and leave before the sun rose again. She had come to offer what support she could. Misty wasn't willing to force her presence on Vera, however, she could support her in other ways. She spent her day catching up with her father until bedtime. She woke early the next morning. Vera hadn't called yet so she'd assumed she had just gone ahead to the interview.

The day seemed to drag on as Misty awaited word from Vera. It was all but afternoon when she'd given up hope. Misty felt her heart breaking for Vera and her family. The double tragedy of the remaining children losing their mother was hard to swallow.

James had a lady friend coming for the evening and Misty wanted to be gone when his company arrived. Her father had been supportive and she thought he deserved to have his house back to enjoy his company. She'd planned to stop and see her brother before she pulled out.

Misty found James sitting on the porch with a beer in hand. She kissed her dad on the forehead and told him she was leaving out. James helped his daughter with her bags to the car. He cautioned her about driving too fast and told her to have a safe trip as she pulled off.

Her dad had once again opened his home to her. She arrived in at nine a.m. When Misty came and got her things settled in; she took a shower and stretched out across the couch. In a matter of minutes she was fast asleep.

When she woke up, Misty went outside and sat in the car. She rolled the window down before she reached into the glove box and took out a fresh pack of cigarettes. Misty lit one and puffed the acrid smoke then blew it out of the open window. She had yet to call Vera either.

The sun had started to set as she looked up toward the sky. The blazing orange ball had faded into subtle a subtle peach color as it faded from view. Misty watched and remembered the day that she'd gotten all the children together and released balloons in the air. She told the kids that it was there way of celebrating Heather's life, just a few years earlier. The same sky that had received the expressions of grief now held her attention as a scene of peacefulness.

Misty heard her dad call out to her. She reluctantly got out of the car and went go see what he wanted. By the time she'd made it to the front door, he passed the receiver of the house phone out to her. Her brow wrinkled as she took the phone.

"Hello" Misty said.

"I just wanted to call you and let you know that this is my last night as a free person. I spoke with my lawyer and he told me to be prepared to go to jail in the morning. I'm going to miss you so much. I'm over here spending some time with the kids right now."

"I'm sorry to hear that. Do you want me to come see you or what?" Misty asked.

"Not right now. I just called to hear your voice one more time. I wish you were here." Vera said.

"It's not the last time you'll hear from me."

Misty heard a loud sound that startled her and then a man shouting through the phone.

"Get on the floor. Put your hands on your head and get down on the floor right now." The man said.

"Vera, what going on, is everything all right?" Misty screamed.

"Okay, okay I'm down." Vera said.

"What going on?" Misty said.

"Where is he?" The man said.

Just then the phone hung up. Misty tried to call back several times but no one answered. In a panic she told James that she'd be back as she ran to the car. Misty wasted little time getting to Vera's house. Several police cars were lined up. The blue and red lights pierced the dark. Misty gripped the steering wheel tightly with one hand while she covered her opened mouth with other.

Chapter 15

Misty drove up a few blocks and parked. She picked up her cell phone from the car seat and scrolled through her contacts. As she hunted for a phone number that Vera had called from prior and hoped the number was to someone who could help. She found the number and pushed dial. When she put the phone to her ear she heard the ring and a man answered on the third ring. She placed her hand on the car door and inhaled, glad someone had answered.

"Hello, this is Misty, I'm a friend of Vera's. Do you know her?"

"Yes, but she's not here right now , is there a message?' the man asked.

"I'm sorry to ask but are you a relative or something to her?"

"Is something wrong?"

"Something's going on at her house, I'm not sure what but I had hoped to get in touch with a relative or something to let someone know."

"Okay, I'll let her Aunt know. Thank you."

"No, thank you."

The phone went dead before she realized that she hadn't gotten a name. She scrolled down the list until she came to the next number she'd thought to call. Base's number lit up and she pushed the button. A southern voice answered on the first ring.

"Hello, Thomas" Misty asked.

"Hello" he replied.

"This is Misty,

"Hey baby, how you doing?"

"How you doing?"

"Good and you?"

"Good, glad to hear."

"Good."

"Ummm huh. Now if I remember correctly you left and planned to travel and see some of your dreams come true, right?"

"Yes, I did."

"Yes lord, music can carry you far. Why when I first fell in love with music I was five years old. My daddy bought me a drum set for Christmas. Had to learn to play them though. My mama helped me. Took me church too, so I could learn to play better. She played the guitar and sang and whatnot. I always did have passion for the beat and harmony, you know. Yeah, love me some music. So you went to College huh? I don't remember getting a invite to your graduation or it's on the way? Let me get me calendar book so I can mark down the date."

"I apologize. I graduated from school quite a few years ago."

"You don't say? That's wonderful, so your got your master's degree. Boy I'll tell music can float a little soul straight through life and generations of time. I'm so proud of you. What's your major?"

"I didn't get my Masters."

"Mm mm huh, well that's excellent, you almost there. Keep up the good work kid. Now how can I help you?"

"I have a friend and I think she's in trouble. Well her kids anyway."

"Kids? In trouble? What's the problem?"

"I don't know exactly but she has a son and I remember that you worked with kids. Whatever is going on their lives on a daily is beyond me, but there's something going on at their house right now. They've been through so much as it, but I'm afraid that they may be lost to the system. I don't live in this state anymore, so my credentials don't help,"

"I got your number. What's the name."

Misty began to recite as much information could recall about the entire family. Thomas was well known and respected for his work with Urban children. By the time they were done, Misty felt much better. She was anxious to hit the road now. Misty had made the decision to go back and pack her things to return to Michigan. The little that she knew might just turn out to be enough for him to help the son, but that didn't really help the girls.

"I can't make you promises, but I'll look into it. Do you know if the boy can play an instrument?" Thomas asked.

"No, I don't." Misty said.

"No matter, a love of music has a way of getting to heart. Sometimes even the most down hearted ones."

"It sure does, Thomas, it sure does."

"You call me and let me know when I need to be there and see you get that masters degree."

"I will"

"No pressure, just you know, keep it on your goal list."

After Misty hung up and pushed a compact disc into the player for her some road music, she pulled out and headed for expressway. As she merged into traffic on I-75 headed toward the Ford freeway interchange, she sighed. Thomas had never known that she fell in love with music by accident. She turned the radio up and decided that she'd never mention it, except to say that it had changed her life.

By the time Misty had made it to I-94 exchange, her cell phone rang again. She'd answered it and smiled when she heard the kids. They'd heard that she'd been in the city and wanted to see her. Misty held the phone. She missed her babies, but was reluctantly to interfere with their newfound happiness. Misty listened to the her children voices and smiled.

Her phone beeped and another call came in. She asked the children to hold on and answered the other call. It was Vera. She informed Misty that everything thing was alright, the police had questioned her and let her go. She still had to make a court appearance but it seemed things would be fine. They'd referred her to some services to help her get on her feet and into a decent place of her own.

Misty told Vera she was glad for her and that she'd call her back. She switched back over and expected to hear the children. Instead, it was Scott. Misty sighed deeply and found a safe place to pull over.

"What Scott?" Misty asked.

"Um before you curse me out. I'm not out to harm you. The children think I can get you to come back to Detroit. You've a beautiful granddaughter and they kids miss you very much. I know I shouldn't be the one asking but if you would please just come back and visit with them. It would me so much to them...and well. Me too." Scott said.

"Scott, I'd love to see them but I'm not anxious to see you at all."

"Okay, I understand. So will you come?"

"My numbers the same. I'll come next weekend and meet them somewhere if they want."

"They want you to come home Misty, they want you to move back to Detroit."

"I'm from Detroit, when I go Detroit, my kids, my family, my heart, my life goes with me in spirit. I'll visit with them and touch base."

"Right now, I think that's more than enough."

Misty phone line beeped once more. She told Scott to have the children call her later. Misty was still parked on the side of the road when she answered. Thomas was on phone.

"Hey" Misty said.

"Listen to my little big headed baby sounding grown. Look, that kid was already in trouble. It's all over the news. Him and few of his friends thought it might be a good idea to jack a minister. I didn't realize you knew any of those kids."

"Oh me either."

"Yeah well listen, he had some family that can look out for him. So that's settled."

"Thank you Thomas, I appreciate it. Listen, my kids…they called me. They sounded different. I'm so happy that but I know that you and dad had something to do with that."

"What? No why would your own family, do anything to see about them kids? That's absurd. What do you take me for. I teach music and love doing it. Why did I every tell you about my first drum set. Dad bought it for me for Christmas, you was too little to remember of course. When I woke up..."

"Thomas, did you?"

"I'd tell you but I feel it's safer if you don't know?"

"What?"

"Yeah, you can't tell what you don't know."

"What the..."

"How are them girls doing? Any news?"

"Ummmm yeah well..."

"Huh, God takes care of fools and babies. I'll talk to you later baby."

"Alright, hopefully at least a few of the younger mother's know now. The most important job you'll ever have is the one God gave you. It ain't always easy, but it's the only one worth it."

"And you know it. The same is true for the men too though. Any fool can get somebody pregnant, but a man put's aside self and cares for them."

"A man that means you some good doesn't want you miserable. He wants a woman that's beside him, not under his boot. It takes a lot to discover and cultivate yourself, but it can be done. I lose my temper, get discouraged, and I know you've been through so much yourself. I'm so happy that he's got it all worked for us. So glad that he's willing to take us higher."

"I agree."

"How's Peach, by the way?"

"As pretty as always, just shining and glowing last time I saw her."

"Mm mm, very good then. Let me get on back to my business then and you go on about yours. Keep in touch."

"For sure, I'll be sure to touch base when I get there."

"You suck at comedy."

"I know…"

Other Works by Inakat

The Synz Series

I Synz En Detroit

II Synz : Remixed and Reloaded January 2013

How Day Getz it Done June 2009

Sasha N. Deeplee March 2011

Smoking Hot Panties (Book 1) October 2012

High Maintenance Assets November 2012

Blog: http://www.realechos.com

Facebook: www.facebook.com/InakatPublishing

Twitter http://www.twitter.com/Inakat1 or @Inakat1

Email: katina@inakat.com

www.ingramcontent.com/pod-product-compliance
Lightning Source LLC
Chambersburg PA
CBHW070606180626
46817CB00005B/2013

9 7 8 0 9 8 8 3 5 3 3 4 3